(a crime drama)
Originally Created - Saturday, April 13, 2024
Updated: Wednesday, July 3, 2024

written by

Denny Magic

©2024 – Brass Belle Literary Publishing
ALL RIGHTS RESERVED

Preface

After penning nearly 80 short-stories and books which are published with **Amazon.com**, I certainly want to thank Jeff Bezos for being my publisher. **As *if* he will ever read this, and appreciate my compliment?**

However, Despite the fact that Amazon and me have had a tremulous relationship over the past 20+ years, regarding the publishing of my short-stories and books. Amazon has never helped me promote my original work in any commercial way!

I am not ungrateful to them for investing the time and money that they have already invested in my work... I certainly do appreciate that.

Of course, there are a lot of hidden expenses for Amazon with each new author that they decide to represent, but if you as a budding author, imagine that Amazon is gonna read your books, and like them enough to spend money trying to promote your work. That is **NEVER** gonna happen if you're not already some sort of celebrity!

In general, I appreciate the fact that Jeff Bezos was willing to publish my work in the first place, especially when other electronic publishers ignored me from day one.

> BTW: Those TV Publishers are useless. Everything that they promise to do [for a brand new author] is attached to some sort of fee that they will charge.

I became an author because one night my late wife leaned back in her chair, in a small office that we shared at home, and suggested that I might possess a decent enough imagination that I should consider becoming a writer.

When I started writing, I had very little knowledge of the English language.

Hell way back then, I openly volunteered [to anyone who would listen] that I could **barely spell**.

My late wife argued that it was my 'storytelling abilities' that mattered, **NOT** my spelling skills.

She was correct!

So, after decades of work, I wanted to be the first to acknowledge that no matter how talented you **THINK** you are, and no matter how **prolific** you try to be... without a big sack of disposable-cash to FUND your writing career from your **Uncle Scrooge**... you will remain an unknown.

Amazon (even if it only involves pennies) will always be the benefactor in the arrangements that you think you have with them.

They're in it for the money (*income*) and they could care less about an unknown and struggling writer like you, or me. They are a business that is supposed to generate profits for their stockholders. I get that.

However, I am still extremely proud to have reached such a level of proficiency as I approach the number of short-stories and books that I have published with Amazon.

Most, so called authors... are lucky to be able to brag about writing just one book.

In fact, I used to love talking with newbie writers who were *bragging about being an author, after writing just one short-story, or book.*

I have said it before... WRITING is certainly one of the <u>loneliest professions in the world</u>. You spend ALL your time working by yourself. The rare exception is when two or more authors' collaborate on the same project.

In most cases, you set yourself up in a room alone with your writing device. No spouse, no phone calls, no pets, no kids, no interruptions of any kind! Just you, a keyboard, and your creative mind.

OK. Maybe some soft music too?

In fact, when I consider all the time that writing took me away from my loving spouse... I do have quite a few regrets. I realize that I 'could have' spent a lot more time with my wife before she passed away... and because of that I do have regrets!

But, every person's situation is completely different.

If you want to write... then become a writer. It CAN be really satisfying... there's no doubt. Which is why there are so, so, many of us.

It's because of my storytelling that I **never** had any REAL desire to take hard-drugs. I was already 'HIGH' on life!

I do take the occasional 'gummy bear' to help me get to sleep at night, but taking drug induced trips so I could *"walk on the wild side"* was never really for me.

As you read this 'crime drama' I hope that you find the story compelling, titillating, and above all, enjoyable.

Regardless of your opinions, <u>one way or another</u>, please consider visiting my website where you can email me your comments.

Your feedback is much more valuable to me, than the meager income a book sale will generate.

Sayonara !

Your feedback is much more valuable to me than the meager income a book sale will generate.

— Djura

Table of Contents

PREFACE	II
OVERDUE REWARD	3
SURPRISE	7
THE BOSS ARRIVES	8
WRAPPING UP HIS WORK OBLIGATIONS	10
PACKING UP	15
CHICAGO, ILLINOIS	23
MORE DETAILS	26
THE BIG MEETING	28
AFTER THE DVD	32
BUTTERFLY LAKE	36
SHOPPING	41
LUNCH	44
THE LAKE	47
GETTING SETTLED IN	52
SETTING UP THE CAMPSITE	56
AFTER DINNER CONVERSATIONS	57
FIRST NIGHT AT BUTTERFLY LAKE	58
BUYING A FEW ESSENTIALS	59
BOREDOM	62
ENTERTAINMENT NIGHT	66
CONTINENTAL BREAKFAST	67
FINDING THE GOLD	76
AT THE AIRPORT	82
FINALLY, THE COPS ARRIVE	85
RELIVING THE DETAILS	87
THE AUTHORITIES TRACK THE CULPRITS	88
ABOUT THE AUTHOR	91

Overdue Reward

Tim Prescott depressed the intercom button to make an announcement to his receptionist, *"Linda can you have Gary Richards step into my office please?"*

"Yes sir, right away." ...Came the voice from the other end.

A few minutes later a junior member of the **Levitt's and Saunders Law Firm** (Gary *Richards*) entered his supervisor's office where he stood there, while Mr. Prescott finished up 'some housekeeping' on his beautiful *Resolution Desk* [just like the desk that sits in the oval office of the White House].

> The desk itself was very impressive in Mr. Prescott's oversized office and was a great PROP that emphasized his importance with the Law Firm! Someday Gary hoped to end up with an impressive office like Mr. Prescott's.

Tim Prescott only took a few moments as he shuffled through the stack of documents, making some room on his desktop. He looked up for a moment and smiled at his employee before pointing at a chair and explaining, *"Please, please... have a seat Gary, give me a few seconds here."*

Gary Richards took a seat and spent some time looking around at the way Mr. Prescott had decorated his office.

Sometimes the way a person decorates their work space can telegraph a lot about their personality.

Gary knew that people usually didn't get a chance to see the inside of Tim Prescott's office unless they were being hired, fired, reprimanded, or complimented.

Gary <u>wasn't confident enough</u> to surmise that he was in Mr. Prescott's office for a compliment. He actually envisioned the worst case scenario.

Gary was admittedly a bit concerned why he'd been called in to see Mr. Prescott. He was a little bit concerned as he waited for Tim to gather his thoughts.

As soon as there was a pause, Gary asked, *"Am I in trouble?"*

Tim laughed. *"My God Gary **NO**, <u>not at all</u>. I hope you find this experience to be a positive one? No. No. Everything is good!"*

Gary mustered up a well needed smile and took a deep breathe. It was the first time that he sat back in the overstuffed leather chair and began to relax as he loosened his grip on the handrails.

Tim smiled before continuing. *"OK. Well... the reason I asked you here today is because of the Belview Lawsuit. Our company made a fortune on that case, thanks to your effort, and the primary reason I called you into my office today, is... the principles want to offer you a full-partnership in the firm."* Tim smiled, waiting for a reaction to his announcement.

Gary was flabbergasted, he looked like a 'deer caught in the headlights'. He was at a loss for words. This was unexpected news.

Everything that he was hearing was a huge surprise and he was **very** unsure that he heard Tim correctly.

Tim picked up where he left off, as he continued to explain, *"AND..."*

Gary could hardly believe his ears, and it was tough to control his smiling face. Then Gary asked, *"You were about to say?"*

Tim Prescott smiled, *"Well, I was about to tell you. They want you to hit the ground running, so... They've authorized a sizable budget for you and your family to spend a month off on a vacation to anywhere in the world that you and your family might like to go. All expenses paid."*

"I don't want to sound ungrateful, Gary paused because he was thrown off kilter... *"But are you talking - the whole family?"* ...As he wasn't too sure that he heard Mr. Prescott correctly.

Tim laughed, *"Of course! of course! You think we'd send you off on an all expense vacation by yourself?"* And he laughed. *"No. No. The whole family is included."*

Gary immediately rubbed his smiling face with his hands! This development was certainly not expected. In fact, he wasn't quite sure what he expected, but this was **NOT** it.

Tim was pleased that this news was quite unexpected for Gary. He had a slight feeling like he was suddenly giving out gifts like Santa Claus.

Of all the tasks that he was asked to perform for the Law Firm... this was indeed one of the most enjoyable kind of meetings that he had in recent weeks.

"When is this all supposed to take place?" ...Gary asked.

Tim picked up a small desk calendar and scrutinized the dates before answering.

"Well, let's see here. Your working on that Safeway Account right now, and eh... when do you think you might wrap that one up?" ...Tim asked.

"Eh, piece of cake. For all intent and purpose the final court case is schedule for the end of the week, my deposition is due, but that's just a formality, limited to the necessary paperwork. Essentially the case has been settled. There's really nothing on my docket after that. I can have everything wrapped up by the end of June. Easily." ...Gary answered.

"So, you and your family could be ready to leave by May?" ...Tim asked.

Gary smiled and nodded in the affirmative.

"OK. Today's Friday so I want you to take the rest of the day off and go home to talk things over with your wife and kids, then when you have an idea where you'd like to go, let me know on Monday and I'll set the wheels in motion."

There was a long silence as Gary struggled to process all this good news.

Tim could see that Gary Richards was in a 'state of shock'. He asked, *"You OK?"*

"More than OK Mr. Prescott!" ...Gary answered.

"Oh, and now that you're a partner in the firm, 'TIM' would be more than adequate from now on. Let's do away with all the formalities." ...Tim added.

It was a long **silent** drive home, as Gary processed his meeting with his **former** supervisor, now his co-worker. He never even turned on the car radio. His mind was racing, and he didn't need any distractions.

5

Surprise

It was close to three in the afternoon.

Gary usually was a guy who NEVER watched the clock and it was highly unusual for him to be arriving home this early as he pulled into his driveway.

When he arrived at his beautiful ranch style five bedroom home in the valley, the primary greeter onsite was the families golden retriever *Chico*.

Chico was noticeably surprised to see Gary's vehicle rolling up the long driveway, arriving so early in the day. Chico was obviously excited to see him.

Gary parked his vehicle in front of the garage and gave Chico a good rub down before making his way into the house where he was greeted by the couples housekeeper (Consuelo) who was quite shocked to see Gary at this time of day.

With all the commotion Consuelo had already followed Chico to the front of the house, to see what Chico was barking about. She was a little bit surprised when she spotted Gary's car. She relaxed and smiled as she stepped out onto the families front porch where she leaned on the railing.

"Mr. G, are you feeling OK?" ...She asked.

Gary smiled and said, *"I'm just fine Consuelo. Actually I'm more than fine. Can you stay with us tonight for dinner, I want you to hear my news for yourself when Maddy and the girls get home."*

"OK Mr. G, just let me call Hugo so he and our son can fend for themselves tonight, regarding dinner.?" ...She explained.

"I hope that your husband will be OK with that?" ...Gary asked.

"Yeah Hugo and my son will be happy to go to McDonalds! Any excuse to go for a Happy-Meal.

They're sick of my cooking anyway." ...She explained with some humor.

Gary said, "*I seriously doubt that!*" And he smiled.

The Boss Arrives

By seven-thirty Gary's wife Madeline (Maddy) rolled up the driveway. She'd spent yet another long day as **the finance administer** over at **Fenway Hospital** where she worked in the accounting department.

It did strike her as odd when she saw her husband's vehicle in the driveway. Gary was usually never home before her and she was worried that something was wrong.

When she saw him, she asked, "*Honey, are you OK?*"

Gary could hardly contain his happiness, and he found it difficult to conceal his smile.

"I'm just fine." He flagged Consuelo and his wife to join him in the living room and he patted the two wingback chairs to encourage both women to take seats. *As everyone was getting situated, he added,* "I had a meeting in Tim Prescott's office today." He looked at Consuelo and tried to clarify his story... "My supervisor." ...Gary explained.

Maddy stopped in her tracks, "Oh, oh... How'd that go?"

Gary had a hard time concealing his emotions, but... when a smile started to spread across his face, he started to explained, "Well. I cannot say that I wasn't a little shocked, but I was."

As Maddy took a seat, she asked. "OK. Tell us? What happened."

Gary looked around waiting for Consuelo to get comfortable before continuing. "My boss, Tim Prescott? Shocked the shit out of me today by offering me a <u>Full Partnership</u> in the firm." ...he revealed.

Maddy and Consuelo broke out in huge smiles and before he could continue Maddy said, "Wow. That's great news honey!"

"I'm happy for you Mr. G!" ...Consuelo responded.

"And there's more." ...Gary interrupted as he continued.

"The firm is sending the whole family on a 'completely paid for' vacation – including the girls - to the destination of our choice, all expenses paid for the entire month of May." ...Gary added.

Then he specifically looked at Consuelo, *"I'd like you to consider being available for that month Consuelo if that's A-OK with you? We'll pay you an extra $500.00 to continue to keep the house up and to keep Chico company while were gone."* ...Gary suggested.

Consuelo smiled, *"Of course Mr. G but paying me extra is not necessary."*

"No. No. It's a small bonus that I'd like to pass along, seeing as you'd be here all by yourself for the month. It would be just you and Chico.

After Chico heard his name, he entered the living room and let out a bark. Everyone laughed.

Wrapping up his work obligations

Gary finished up his obligations at work as he made ready to leave for the entire month of May.

> *Maddy had loads of accumulated vacation time saved up at the hospital... and it was fairly easy for her to take a break from work, so she made all the necessary arrangements for the family's time off.*

She managed to secure the entire month of May off plus one extra week, before... they left town.

She took the extra week off at the end of April, and she pulled both daughters <u>out of school</u> a week early to help her get the family up-to-speed so they could enjoy their time away from home without too many worries. Consuelo help the family get organized.

Maddy, the girls, and Consuelo all worked together, to make sure that the family had the necessary luggage, clean clothes, and accouterments that they would need while they were away from home.

> *Gary continued to go to work every day to wrap up his obligations at the firm.*

During that time, Maddy and the girls also made the rounds to the local pet supply to ensure that Consuelo had everything that Chico might need as well.

She double checked to make sure that Consuelo had all the emergency telephone numbers like the local Vet for Chico, and the alarm company including everything that might be necessary in their absence.

Of course that included a few boxes of Chico's favorite... **Milk Bones** from Chewy®.

Chico had put on quite a bit of weight because Consuelo was feeding him Milk Bones at every opportunity throughout the day.

The more she gave him, the more he consumed. And he was gaining weight because of the affection that she felt for him.

That night at the dinner table, the family FINALLY sat down to a nice meal that Consuelo had prepared. That's when the subject of 'where they all agreed to go' came up.

As the family enjoyed yet another fantastic meal prepared by Consuelo, they FINALLY began to discuss where they would spend their vacation.

Melanie and Rachel (the couple's twin daughters) were the first to broach the subject. Mel spoke up first, *"So dad, where are YOU & MOM wanting to go on our vacation?"*

"Well. Your mother and I thought that we'd like to hear from you two girls about that first?" ...Gary asked.

Melanie glanced at her sister and smiled. *"Well. Rach and I were thinking... You know, we're both glued to the TV when that Gold Rush Series is on television?"*

Maddy was about to pass the mashed potatoes and she almost dropped the entire bowl when Mel said that.

"Are you and you sister serious? That's just some baloney TV series." ...Their mother announced.

Rach jumped right into the conversation to try to correct her mother , *"Mom it's a reality series based on facts. That guy Parker Schnabel is a real person like us, it's not fiction. Besides none of us have ever been to Alaska."*

Gary was slightly disappointed by the girls suggestion. And he spoke up, *"What about a place like Yosemite, or Yellowstone? We could camp out and enjoy the wilderness."*

Both twins said exactly the same thing at the same time, "CAMPING?"

Maddy recognizing the girls response, spoke up. *"What's wrong with camping?"*

Mel gave her mother a 'look' only a disgruntled teenager could provide. "Mother, please. Camping is so 1950's!"

Then Maddy asked her, *"How can you pass judgement that quickly, you've never even been camping?"*

Mel responded, *"Not since you sentenced Rach and me to that tent in the backyard when we were just impressionable children."*

"Oh come on Mel, you loved it!" ...Maddy replied.

Rach added, *"You didn't have to spend the night in that thing. It wasn't any fun for us! We were scared stiff!"*

Maddy was a bit shocked, and looked over at Gary who was hearing about this for the first time, before he finally added. *"I thought that you girls enjoyed that experience?"*

Mel chimed in, *"Well if we spent the night in a tent at our current age, it wouldn't have been so traumatic dad. But we were just two little girls."*

Maddy responded, *"Hummmm, Well if your father and I made a mistake, I'm sorry Mel. We were only trying to entertain you girls. Besides, you were only fifty feet away from the safety of the house. If something was to happen, you could have easily taken shelter inside."*

Mel responded, *"Easy for you to say NOW. For all we knew, the house was locked."*

Gary chimed in, *"Let me see if I understand... You think that we forced you to sleep in the backyard in a tent, and that we, as your parents... locked our two kids out of the house?"*

Rach added, *"OK. OK. I guess you didn't actually lock the back door, but..."*

Gary then asked. *"So that's why you two are opposed to camping?"*

"Look dad, we are not opposed to camping, it's just that you asked our opinions about where we want to go, that's all." ...Mel clarified.

Then she added, "Rach and I have done quite a bit of research on the internet, and there's a third-party-company that runs bus tours out to the mining site for the Gold Rush TV show. And when the TV production team isn't shooting an episode they allow people to visit the site, and on occasion... some of the cast members from the show are rumored to make possible guest appearances to meet the public."

"Alaska huh?" ...Gary asked.

The twins both nodded in agreement.

"So if we agree to go to Alaska, will you both agree that you'll spend some of your time camping out with your mom and me?" ...Gary asked.

The girls seemed to consult silently with one another, and after nodding their heads in unison, they answered simultaneously like only twins are prone to do, "Yes."

Mel added, "Against my better judgement, I guess we'll agree to go camping. But **NO FISHING**!"

"Whoa. I might like to try my luck fishing." ...Rach added.

"Are you serious Rach? You fishing?" ...Mel asked her sister in amazement. Then she added. "Whose gonna bait the hook for you? You gonna do that? A person who is deadly afraid of anything that crawls on its belly?" ...Mel asked.

"Well, if dad finds us a decent place to camp and fish, then he ought to have a chance to see me catch my first fish?" ...Rach pronounced.

"*Hey, that's the spirit!*" ...Gary responded.

Mel rubbed her forehead in disbelief before giving her sister a dirty look. She added, *"Traitor!"*

Everyone at the table laughed.

Packing Up

So as that week came to a close, Mel, Rach, and Maddy (with Consuelo's help) seemed to have purchased everything that they 'may' have needed for their family vacation. And everything was packed up into a small rental trailer.

The trailer was looking like a small sporting goods store. Of course there were things packed in the trailer that they would probably never touch during their entire trip, but... if worse came to shove... like a **zombie apocalypse**... they would have something in the trailer that would come in handy, even for that!

Reluctantly, Maddy and Gary agreed that they would allow the girls to book a seat on the "Gold Rush" Tour-Bus. In return, the girls made the commitment and agreed to go camping. That was the trade-off!

Gary and Maddy were on the computer every night attempting to locate a destination in Alaska that was conveniently located within a few miles of the "Gold Rush Tour" for the convenience of the girls.

Gary and Maddy knew that the Alaskan Yukon was NOT too close of a match to a vacation at Yellowstone, or Yosemite... But, neither of them had ever set foot in Alaska and because they didn't want a new problem to arise between them and their girls... They accepted the girl's vacation suggestion with a grain of salt.

Regardless of the location this might end up being the last time the entire family would be together and Gary and his wife knew this... so they capitulated.

Gary thought to himself how his twins had gotten their way. <u>Again</u>. It was obvious that the two girls had conspired once again to manipulate their parents into getting what **they** wanted.

But Gary and Maddy understood the importance of this vacation in more ways than one.

With Gary's work schedule this vacation was a much needed reward for the long hours and commitment that he had made to the law firm over the years.

Besides, soon the twins would be off to college and he wondered if this vacation might be the last family event where they could all be together.

He recalled the few times that he sat through an episode of "Gold Rush" with the girls... He was reminded how stunning the Alaskan countryside really was.

The "Gold Rush" location per say, was **NOT** an attractive representation of the true beauty of Alaska, and Gary knew that, but being fairly close to the Gold Mining town of Dawson City, the general location did offer some local history, and because the locals had kept Dawson City as close to its original appearance as possible they city planners had managed to capture its rustic *Old West* charm.

Despite the charm of Dawson City, the actual Gold Mining site was *NOT* much to look at. The ground was chewed up by heavy duty equipment and the actual mining location was certainly nothing much to look at.

It was torn up as episodes of the TV show will attest, and the scattered trailers that the Cast & Crew lived in at the site when the series was being filmed... gave it a kind of *'corporation yard'* feel. The encampment was certainly nothing to write home about.

There wasn't a vast expanse of beauty onsite because the guys on the show were digging up the entire countryside. Although the surrounding mountains and forests remained gorgeous.

Beautiful, majestic mountains surrounded the site punctuated by rolling tree-covered hills that seemed to be heavily populated with local wildlife.

It was some of that wildlife that motivated the production crew, and the miners to keep a few firearms handy.

Black Bears, Wolves, and Moose were abundant in the area, and those animals COULD be a problem from time to time.

Fire was also a very real threat, and because of that... any mining team *'worth their salt'*, had a 'safe spot' located a safe distance from the main camp that was designated as a spot to retreat to in case of catastrophe. The mining camp had a small shed that provided canned food, medical supplies, and a small generator that could run an emergency satellite radio to call for help... just in case any problems arose.

Some fans of the series probably wondered if mining operations such as this one, would be conscientious enough to return the countryside back to its pristine condition after they had taken everything that they wanted from the soil?

In fact Gary hoped (and he said so... in front of his girls) that the miners should be good stewards of the land?

He didn't know where the girls got their information from, but they spoke up immediately when he expressed his concerns, saying, *"Yes. There were laws in Alaska that mandated that when the miners were done extracting as much gold from the ground as possible. That they were required by law to return the land back to the way that they found it."*

If the miners actually 'owned' their claim, the local government could only impose a 'bare-bones-policy of conservatism... as a request.

But, the producers' of the series knew that IF a proper 'clean up' didn't happen... permission to film the show would come to a screeching halt. No one wanted that to happen, so everyone on the filmed series was on their best behavior.

However, the big names in the Gold Rush saga (especially those that appeared on TV every week) had to set examples as good stewards of the land.

At least… if the producers wanted to be able to renew the series from year to year? Filming permits were hard to come by and coveted by everyone on the show.

Of course there were always certain unscrupulous individuals that wanted to 'bend the rules', but those folks were not 'principal players' who appeared on the TV every week.

Part of the job that the producers had to contend with was 'who the claim owners hired, and who they fired.' Sometimes transient workers who were just passing through did not set the best examples. But those folks didn't last long.

Those people were ONLY interested in the money and could care less about how they left the surrounding countryside. And those folks were usually sent home early.

The producers also had to help negotiate the weekly stipend that was paid out to anyone who appeared **on screen**, which included medical insurance and other typical 'employer expenses' that were associated with the running of ANY business.

As the departure date drew closer, Gary was relegated to inspecting the packing of their vehicle, while they were packing the trailer, he asked his daughter Rachael, *"By the way, How much are the tickets for that "Gold Rush" bus tour anyway?"*

"They're fairly reasonable."… Rach answered.

Gary stopped in his tracks. *"How much is 'reasonable'?"*

"They're only $75.00 each for kids under 21 and $150.00 for each Adult." …she answered.

This brought Gary to a stand-still! He frowned and took a long look at his daughters blatant disregard for money. *"You think $300.00 for two teenaged girls is reasonable?"*

"Well. That's reasonable, when you consider that the bus picks everyone up somewhere near Dawson City and it's approximately an hour's drive just to get out to the Dominion Creek Claim that Parker Schnabel's Crew is working." ...She answered.

Then Rach asked. *"Does this mean that you and mom have an interest in coming along with us?"*

*"That would be $600.00 for all four of us honey. No. No. I think you and your sister can go on your own... Your mom and me don't need to spend that kind of money just to gawk at a bunch of construction workers driving around heavy duty equipment. Even if they **ARE** on TV."* ...Gary reasoned.

He paused for a moment. *"Do you even get an opportunity to meet **The Cast** for the price of a ticket?"*

Rach stopped working and walked over to where her father was standing, "The tour company did speculate that maybe, <u>at least one</u> of the recognizable TV Cast could greet the bus and give us a 25¢ Tour of the site. But the tour company was quick to point out that 'meeting a cast member, was unlikely. In all likelihood it was entirely possible that cast members might not be there at all."

"Look Rach, if we were to spend $600.00 I'd want the entire cast to roll out the red carpet when we arrived! I mean, the people on that bus should be able to meet the entire cast, don't you think? Maybe the tourist's should be in an episode?" ...Gary said sarcastically, before laughing out loud sarcastically.

Rach shook her head at her father's sarcasm. "*You're too much dad. It's an opportunity, even if it's just a few of the people who are on TV every week, show up?*"

Maddy had stepped out to the families' driveway with a few items that needed to be packed. Then she asked, "*Whose on TV?*"

"*Rach was trying to explain that for six hundred bucks that we could ride in a cramped bus for over an hour to some remote gold mining operation just so we can look at a hole in the ground and meet some guy's from that Gold Rush TV Show.*" ...Gary sarcastically explained.

"*Guy.*" Rach corrected him. "*It might just be one guy, dad.*"

He threw his arms up into the air, "*Just one guy? What's wrong with the kids today. Hell, when your mother and me were teenagers we were able to see The Rolling Stones at the Oakland Coliseum in concert for fifty bucks a ticket! How come you and your sister aren't hounding me for tickets to see that Taylor Snit instead?*"

"**Swift** *Dad. And good seats for one of her shows would have cost you a heck of a lot more than that for a single seat, dad. Maybe a lot closer to a thousand bucks per ticket?*" ...She argued.

Gary sarcastically added, "For a thousand bucks, I'd want to see Jesus Christ himself." And he shook his head in disbelief, before adding, "*OK. OK. Just be careful as you freely spend our money, OK?*"

He packed up one of the family's pieces of luggage in the trailer, then he suddenly stopped to ask. "What if you have to pee? I mean, is there a restroom on that bus?"

"Dad. I don't think so? But for crying out loud pop, We'll be in the middle of Alaska. I'm sure the driver will make some pit stops along the way?" ...She added.

Because Maddy had just arrived at the trailer and only heard the tail end of the conversation, she asked, "Well, maybe you and your sister should take some toilet paper with you, just in case? Huh?"

Rach could only shake her head, "OK mom. We'll throw a roll in one of our back packs."

Maddy added, "And be sure to bring your iPhones."

Gary shook his head, "Honey, they ain't gonna have any cell phone service way the hell out there."

Then he asked. "Will the bus driver have some sort of satellite radio in case something bad happens?"

At that moment Mel pulled out a brochure from the tour company, "It says here that the driver will definitely have a Satellite Phone, and if something really bad happens, he or she can call for a helicopter."

As Gary continued packing the vehicle, he spoke under his breathe, "Oh great! Just what we need... a $1,000.00 an hour fuel bill for a fricken helicopter, let's hope that nothing bad happens!"

Maddy smiled at Gary's obvious concerns and she sarcastically asked, "What? To the cost of a helicopter or something else?"

The bottom line was that she was pleased that this rare vacation would be enjoyed by her entire family.

Then she asked, *"Did your father tell you girls that we found a nice, picturesque spot just outside Dawson City called 'Butterfly Lake'"*.

The girls smiled, and Mel asked, *"You have any pictures?"*

Gary answered, *"Tonight, I'll bring it up on the computer, so you girls can see where you'll be spending you prison time!"*

Maddy shook her head at her husbands attempt to be funny.

Chicago, Illinois

In Champaign, Illinois at a small apartment in the suburbs the telephone rang.

Peter Schmidt stepped over to where his iPhone was laying on the kitchen table. He answered. *"This is Peter."*

There was a short pause before he smiled. ***"Scorpio!*** *You were the last person that I expected to return my call."*

A voice at the other end spoke through the phone, and Peter listened. Then he interrupted, *"Yes. Yes. I'm willing to pop for some upfront cash. No problem."*

The voice at the other end apparently asked, and Peter answered, *"Is $5,000.00 enough?"* the voice at the other end seemed to agree.

There was a question and Peter responded. *"Yes. We're meeting at my place on Saturday around two."* The person at the other end asked who else had signed up?

*"Look Sabrina... eh **Scorpio**, sorry. Come to the meeting on Saturday and you'll have a chance to meet everyone. I'm attempting to keep everyone's 'real' name off my iPhone, that's all."*...He tried to explain.

The person at the other end said something... Then Peter responded, *"No. My phone is not tapped, I'm just trying to be cautious that's all."*

There was a pause while the caller asked a question, Peter responded, *"OK. Great. Saturday at 2 PM. See ya."*

Peter hung up and sat the phone back down on the kitchen table. He turned towards his living room where another guy was patiently waiting on his couch. Peter announced, *"OK. **Scorpio** will be here on Saturday!"*

*The guy sitting on Peter's couch asked, "What the fuck is all this **Scorpio** shit?"*

"Did you ever see that movie **Reservoir Dogs**?" Peter tried to explain... and the guy on the couch nodded. "Well, now that Sabrina is calling herself **Scorpio**, I thought that I'd ask everyone to come up with a name that we can use that is unrecognizable by anyone on the team." ...Peter explained.

The guy on the couch shook his head and added, "This is a heist, not some new super hero comic book!"

"OK. OK. Fred. But we need to be cautious that's all, I'm just saying." ... Peter tried to reason with him.

Fred spoke up, "OK. You can call me **Fool**. I hope that you can explain things fully on Saturday, because I am already starting to feel fool-ish."

"Peter smiled. "Trust me, making a name change is the least of your worries. After we pull this heist off, you can afford to call yourself anything that you want."

Fred looked at Peter with one-eye open. He was obviously cautious, and not entirely sure that he was part of this one. But, he did ask. "You gonna front me five grand too?"

Peter nodded his head, "Yeah. OK. I guess everyone is gonna put the pinch on me for 5K. Jesus Christ, I'm putting up all the fucking money for everything. I've got a closet full of weapons in there, that already cost me a fucking fortune (he pointed to an adjacent room) I've got the best that money can buy, can you trust me on that one?"

"Look Peter, I'm your friend, and I'm interested... But I just did 12 years at Riker's Island because of a heist that went wrong. A heist that the organizer said couldn't possibly go wrong."

"Look Fred," ...

Fred corrected him, '**Fool**'.

"Yeah right, '**Fool**'... Look these things can go south sometimes, but when they go right... the payoff can be enormous." ...Peter added.

"Yeah, well... I sat in a 6' x 9' cell for12 years wondering what went wrong, while the guy that came up with that idea never spent a single day in the joint." ... '**Fool**' pointed out.

Peter did not have any reasonable response. Then He said, "Come on let's get a bite to eat, my treat!" And the two men left Peter's apartment.

More Details

At the restaurant Peter tried to educate '**Fool**' with some additional details. "*You remember that armored car heist that happened a couple of decades ago in the U.K., the one where they made off with [according to the police reports] around eight million British pounds?*"

"Yeah, yeah, sure. What about it?" ...'**Fool**' responded.

Peter offered some additional details, "I don't want to give away too much here. But on Saturday when we have everyone in the same room, I'll lay out the game plan. For now, enjoy your lunch. Suffice it to say, this heist will be worth a hell of a lot more! And the cash will be 100% untraceable."

'**Fool**' could not contain his glee, and he broke out in a great big grin. Then he asked, "*You mentioned weapons? What about the law?*"

Peter looked around the restaurant nervously and said, "Keep your voice down."

Then '**Fool**' continued in almost a whisper, "I mean I'm not opposed to killing a few civilians if this thing is gonna be worth it and it suddenly goes south, so I'm gonna assume that you spent some time thinking things through?"

"I've been researching this one for more than a year my man." ...Peter explained. Then he added, "Look let's enjoy our lunch and on Saturday, I'll reveal all the details." ...as Peter tried to change the subject.

The Big Meeting

On Saturday a Motley Crew showed up right on time and once everyone was seated Peter began to address the gaggle of seasoned crooks.

"OK. I've been researching this 'job' for a long, long, time and there is no doubt that it's doable." ...Peter explained.

One of the men who had not been introduced yet asked, *"Risks?"*

"Excuse me?" ...Peter asked.

"Risks? What are the fucking risks?" ... the unknown man asked.

"I think the risks are not much different from anything that any of you have taken part in, in the past." ...Peter tried to explain before being interrupted by a third guy who also had not been introduced as of yet.

But before that fellow could speak, Peter said, "OK. First let me establish our alias's. If you all recall that Quentin Tarantino movie, '**Reservoir Dogs**'?

Everyone sitting around the room shook their heads and chuckled.

"Well, as silly as it may sound **Scorpio** here and **Fool** have adapted new names, and as this thing comes together, I'd like everyone to adapt an alias. From this point forward, everyone will use their alias and at no time will any of us use our real names when speaking to each other. Savvy?" ...Peter demanded.

One of the unnamed men smiled and spoke up, "Oh, like Mr. Pink?" Everyone in attendance laughed.

"Yes. Exactly. None of us have ever worked together, so unless you've already revealed your real name to each other... Your identities will remain anonymous." ...Peter explained.

Then he added. "So, from now on we **ONLY** use our fake names."

The Caucasian fellow who spoke up earlier, chimed in... "Ok everyone, I'm taking **Mr. Pink**."

The man of color spoke up... "Well, I guess it'll be obvious that I'll be **Mr. Black**."

The group was silent... "What?" ...**Mr. Black** asked."

No one said a word.

Mr. Pink asked Peter, "What are we supposed to call you?"

"Because I'm the architect of this operation, and because I won't be present during the actual heist. You all can me..." He thought about it for a brief moment and finally said, "**The Architect**." ...Peter suggested.

Pink spoke up, "Did you pick that name because you're the brains behind everything?" ...He asked.

Peter contemplated **Pink's** statement. "Well, yeah. It's befitting don't-cha think?"

Scorpio jumped into the conversation, "Because he's bringing the whole crew together and paying all the upfront expenses, he can call himself anything that he wants. I'm good with that! Let's move on shall we?"

Black added, "Look I don't give a shit what any of you call yourself, but I like the idea. **Black** is just fine with me. So 'Peter' what's to stop us from cutting you out of this deal altogether." ...**Black** asked.

Then he added as a backhanded apology. *"I mean, if you're not a part of the actual heist, why would you trust everyone to make sure that you get a share?"*

Peter wasn't too pleased with the tone of that and he quickly responded, *"Because I've been learning how to fly a helicopter for the past three years, and I'll be your ticket home when we have the prize. Without that Helicopter, you'll never get out of the area. I'm planning to fly in and pick all of you up once we pull this thing off."*

Scorpio jumped in, *"Count me in."* ...She looked around at the others waiting for a similar commitment.

Then she added, *"Obviously Peter, eh...* **Architect** *has invested a lot of upfront money and time planning this heist, so show him some respect."*

Black seemed somewhat reluctant, *"Helicopter? Shit man, I don 't know about that? I'm not too fond of helicopters since I was shot down in one in Viet Nam. I don't know, man?"*

Pink smiled and spoke up, *"Man up, you pussy. Let's hear what* **Architect** *has to say before we all start bailing."* Then he added, *"It kind of sounds like we're gonna be at some remote site."*

"Yes. Good call. We're going into the wilderness in Alaska. We'll be in a remote area about an hour's drive from the nearest town. The local jurisdiction doesn't have a budget for their own helicopter, so it's unlikely that the cops will be able to respond before we all fly away. But there's always the possibility that there might be a small army onsite and they're well-armed! Mostly because of the local wildlife. That means that there will be no shortage of guns. Then there's the Satellite Phones that do exist on site, so the long arm of the law is probably gonna be made aware of what's happening as it goes down."

Pink asked, "So how are we supposed to get anything of value way the hell out in some remote location. And what the fuck are we going after? I mean, what makes this job 'worth it?'"

Everyone sitting in **Architect's** apartment was silent as they waited patiently for an answer.

Architect smiled confidently. *"Gold."*

Architect reached over and picked up a DVD from the kitchen table. *"I think that after you watch this video, you'll start to understand why this is gonna be the biggest heist in history."*

"For Christ's sake **Architect** , I didn't come all the way out here to watch some fricken video." ... **Pink** spoke. The others all seemed to agree.

Pink spoke, "Hey. Shut the fuck up! If you don't like the movie, **LEAVE**! Otherwise, let's give **Architect** the benefit of a doubt."

"**Black** added, "OK. OK. Put the fricken movie on!"

After the DVD

Pink is shocked and speaks up again, *"Jesus Christ, did I hear that guy correctly?"*

Architect smiled, *"You did!"* Then he explained. *"This particular mining crew has been super successful and it's estimated that there's an enormous stash of raw gold in their safe, amounting to Millions of Dollars in value."*

Pink interrupted. *"OK. I've heard enough, I'm outta here."* ...And he tried to stand up, when **Black** grabbed his arm to restrain him.

"Wait a minute." ...**Black** said. *Then he looked at* **Architect** *and asked, "So IF everything goes as planned what in the fuck are we supposed to do with a bunch of gold? I mean it's not like we can walk into a store for something and try to pay with a zip lock bag full of gold?"*

"That's a good question **Black**." ... **Architect** responded, then he continued. "WHEN we make our escape [with the gold] I've already made all the arrangements with a connection that I have in Saudi Arabia. My connection is willing to pay 85% of the current value per ounce. All we need to do is to transfer the gold to a private jet that will be waiting at the airport when I land the chopper. While we're over water, we can dump the weapons and anything else that might link us to the heist." ... **Architect** explained.

Scorpio chimed in, "What about a flight plan for the chopper? You're gonna have to file a flight plan? Once the cops find out about us making our escape in a chopper they'll be on this like stink-on-shit?

"**Architect** was certainly under some growing pressure to explain more of the details, "I understand your concern, But I already have a good relationship with the Saudi's who I've already worked with on some other jobs successfully, and they have proven themselves greedy enough that I know that they can be trusted."

Then he added, "Plus, I've already paid off lessor players to help us <u>buy some time at the airport</u>.

Once the gold is transferred to the waiting jet, and they take off... We're clean. No weapons, no gold, not a single thing that can be traced back to the crime scene. We're off scott free!

Then **Architect** added, "There won't be a damned thing that would link us to this crime except our independent names, and faces so please... get used to using your aliases? And once all of you are paid your share, you'll need to make yourselves as scarce as hell. But the payoffs will allow you to disappear."

Then **Architect** continued, "*The Saudi's will transfer the designated payoff to each of you in a special account with an offshore Deutsch Bank. After that, you all can do whatever you want with the money. You can go anywhere in the world to live, with no one the wiser.*" **Architect** explained.

Black asked, "*You actually trust those Saudi bastards?*"

"*Look. I've been working on this one for a long time now. Yes. The Saudi's are crooked, but we're talking about millions of tax free income here. Trust me, they're already interested in cooperating.*"
…**Architect** explained.

With that said, everyone even the reluctant **Pink** who seemed to waver, were now on board.

Pink asked, "*You said that you will supply all the weapons?*"

Architect smiled, "*I have brand new 9mm Uzi's that the Saudi's helped me acquire from Israel, along with 18 round Glocks for everyone. You'll be issued at least six magazines that are interchangeable and can be used in both weapons.*

Black asked, "*So, if push comes to shove, we may have to kill a few civilians?*"

Architect responded, "*Yes. If necessary? You may have to knock off a few bystanders just to get their attention.*"

The group became silent as they pondered what he just said. **Architect** wasn't too keen to see everyone clam up. "*Anyone have a problem with that?*"

Pink seemed a bit stressed, and he asked, "*What if there are kids present?*"

The group seemed to be looking at one another for each other's response, and then **Scorpio** interrupted the silence, *"Fuck it, I'm in!"*

Then each crook began to follow suit, one at a time.

Architect smiled, *"OK. Good. I want to meet next Tuesday evening and I'll go over the plan in more detail. Can everyone make that meeting?"*

Everyone nodded.

Then **Architect** smiled, *"OK see you next Tuesday around 7 pm."*

The group started to stand up and leave one by one.

Scorpio was the last to vacate and she said, *"God damn, what a bunch of fucking pussies. You'd think that they want to live forever? I'm excited!"*

Architect smiled and patted her on the shoulder, *"Great. Welcome to the team."*

She smiled, and suggested, *"Want to get something to eat?"*

Architect responded, *"You think that would be appropriate?"*

"Look I'm not asking you to sleep with me, I'm just a little famished that's all." ...**Scorpio** clarified.

Architect felt silly for insinuating a possible sexual encounter [in her mind] and he capitulated, *"Yeah OK. I could stand a decent meal, come on, my treat."* And the two of them left **Architect's** apartment.

Butterfly Lake

The drive north to Alaska was long and arduous especially for Gary and Maddy's two girls. They knew better, but both girls deferred to that aged old phrase over and over again, *"Ae we there yet?"*

Despite the cranky comments from their two girls, they made several stops along the way to pee and to get a bite to eat at well-established tourist destinations.

They did manage to see Crater Lake and along the way they stayed in a plethora of flea bag motels, and everyone was thrilled to death to finally arrive in Dawson City in the Alaskan Territories.

Dawson City had preserved the quaint western décor that people associated with the Gold Rush which made the little city very interesting to everyone who visited.

Of course Maddy and the two girls went shopping as soon as they could escape the confines of the car, while Gary roamed the town on his own.

Gary was extremely interested in the history of the area, and while he was roaming freely he purchased a map of the area, and he even stopped in a local watering hole *"Gus Fiddler's Saloon"* to see if he could pick the brain of any locals that might be able to help guide him and his family to *Butterfly Lake*.

He approached the bartender wo was a sight-to-see all by himself.

He had two grey hair braids that ran all the way down his back to his ass, along with a long beard that reached half way down his chest. His name tag said Bradley "Harry" Morehouse (like the mustard).

"Hi Mr. Morehouse"...Gary announced.

"Hello stranger. It's just Harry. We're not too formal around here especially at 'The Fiddler'"... he emphasized.

"Eh, OK Harry, can I get a shot of wild turkey?" ...Gary asked while making himself comfortable on a bar stool.

"Eighty or a hundred?" ...Harry immediately asked.

Gary was a bit confused as he was taking a long look around the saloon at the décor and the mix of the motley crew that permeated the bar. He asked, *"Ah, 80 or 100?"*

Harry smiled, *"Proof? Eighty or a hundred proof?"*

Gary laughed at his inability to decipher what Harry was getting at. *"Oh eh, 80 would be more than adequate."*

And Harry reached for a bottle off the shelf behind him. He grabbed a shot glass and poured Gary his drink.

Gary smiled and reached for the glass.

"You want me to run a tab, or... You wanna just pay as ya go?"... Harry asked.

Gary was a bit embarrassed that he wasn't prepared to pay, so he reached for his wallet and pulled out a twenty, carefully sliding it closer to Harry who snatched it up and turned towards the cash register to add it to the day's take. In a brief moment he slapped Gary's change back on the bar.

Before Harry could leave to attend to another customer, Gary brought out the map that he had purchased earlier and as he unfurled it in front of him on the bar, he asked, *"Harry how close might I be to Butterfly Lake?"*

Harry leaned over putting both hands on the bar, and then he pointed across the room to a huge buckskin clad man with a coon skin hat sitting by the window, *"See that feller over there in the buckskin? He lives up that way. Your questions about Butterfly Lake can be best answered by him."*

Then he stood up erect and whistled... which brought the entire bar to a silence before he yelled to the guy sitting at the table across the room. *"Hey Squeezle? This fella needs some information about the Butterfly, can you help him?"*

Once the guy sitting at the table heard from Harry, he motioned for Gary to come over with his outstretched hand... then he dragged a bent back chair from another table closer to his table with his foot, for Gary to sit on. And he patted the seat with his enormous appendage.

Gary smiled and folded up his map, grabbed his drink and made his way over to converse with this fellow.

When he arrived he smiled and took a seat in the chair that this fellow had dragged over to his table.

As Gary sat down he reached out to shake hands with this enormous guy who he estimated must have been well over six feet tall and certainly close to 350 lbs. He looked like an actor from some Mountain Man Movie, but he seemed to be as gentle as a pussy cat.

Gary was surprised at this guy's enormous size, and as they shook hands he realized how his *'little lawyer hand'* was almost invisible as they shook to greet each other. He thought to himself, 'What a character. Right out of the Old West.'

"What can I help you wid stranger?" ...Squeezle asked.

Gary introduced himself, *"Mr. Squeezle, my name's Gary Richards and I'm up here vacationing with my wife and two girls."*

At that point Gary began to open the map that he had purchased, *"I eh, I was hoping that you could help me locate the best way to get to Butterfly Lake?"*

Squeezle laughed and reached over and grabbed the map from Gary's hands which Gary had just started to unfurl. *"Well. Lemme see that damned thing. Eh, ah, OK you be right here and this here's Butterfly Lake. I hope you're only going up there to see the sights for the day, because since the government took over the running of the campground, you gotta have reservations if you want to camp there. Damned bureaucrats mess everything up once they get their fingers in the pie, you know?"*

"Oh yeah, my wife and me made arrangements on the computer to get a campsite for the next couple of weeks. At least I hope that somebody there confirmed our reservations?" ... Gary related.

"Are you one of those computer geeks" ...Squeezle asked.

"No actually I'm a lawyer, but I'm computer savvy." ...Gary remarked.

Squeezle made a face, "I hate those fricken computers. What a waste of time!" ...and he shook his head in disbelief. "Ain't got much use for lawyers either. No offense?"

Gary smiled and took a look around the room, "Yeah, I wouldn't think so."

Squeezle motioned with his outstretched fingers, "You got sumtin' to write wid?" and Gary retrieved a ball point pen from his breast pocket allowing Squeezle to continue. "OK. You be right here right now" and he made an X on the location where 'The Fidler' is located, "And you be wantin' to go here," and he drew a second X on the edge of the lake pictured on Gary's map. "So, just follow my marks and you'll find it." He paused for a second. "When you get there, they have a fancy registration building now, and when you arrive, go there first... and they can git you to whatever spot you're gonna be bedding down at."

Then Squeezle looked at Gary's Glass, "Whatcha drinking?" But before Gary could answer, Squeezle looked over towards Harry, and motioned using sign language for another beer for himself, and another shot for his new friend.

Gary tried to pass on that second shot, but Squeezle ignored him.

Harry poured another shot of wild turkey for Gary, and he drew a mug of draft for Squeezle. Then he walked the two drinks over to Squeezle's table.

Immediately Gary said, "You didn't have to buy me a drink my friend."

Squeezle took a huge drink of his beer almost drinking half of it in one gulp, wiping his mouth on his buckskin sleeve before answering. *"I didn't. These drinks are on your tab my friend, in exchange for all the valuable information I be giving to you."*

Gary could only smile and he nodded his head. He wasn't about to argue with this fellow, and he accepted the terms like a lawyer who'd just lost a case.

He thanked this fellow for the information and after downing his second shot of wild turkey he made his way out to the main street.

He was a bit hungry and was interested in finding his wife and daughters. He was also noticeably inebriated.

Shopping

Maddy and their two daughters were caught up in the appeal of shopping, something all women seem to love.

They were pre-occupied when Maddy noticed Gary walking on the wooden sidewalk just across the street, from the dress shop that they were in.

"There's your father, girls!"...She commented.

Mel and Rach momentarily took a break from roaming the shop to gawk out the window at their father, then they immediately went back to the shopping experience. It was obvious which issue was more important to them at the moment.

Maddy saw Gary stumble a little as his shoe caught on an errant piece of planking on the boardwalk, and she mumbled to herself, *"Oops! Is your father drunk?"*

And she set her purchases down on a showcase and turned towards her daughters. *"You girls stay right here... I'm going to speak to your father. I'll be right back."* And she left the dress shop.

The girls hardly acknowledged her comment other than a simultaneous (uninterested) *"Um Hum."* They never lost a beat in their shopping endeavors.

Maddy crossed the street as she tried to get her husband's attention. *"Honey?"*

Gary smiled and took a seat on a bench that was conveniently located in front of an ice cream shop. Maddy sat down next to him. *"You OK? I saw you stumble back there."*

Gary looked around to make sure that no one was listening then he said. *"Aw shit, my shoe caught on a nail or something that's all."*

Maddy sniffed the air. *"You've been drinking? Haven't you?"*

"Well. I was commiserating with the locals, that's all, and yeah I had a couple of drinks." ...Gary reluctantly admitted.

She sat back and asked, *"Did you find out anything useful?"*

Gary laughed, "Well I met the local bartender, a guy named Harry, and he IS... Harry that is! He has a double pony tail that runs all the way down to his ass."

He took a huge breath before continuing, "But Harry did introduced me to another character named Squeezle. That guy was all decked out in buckskin. He even had a coon skin hat on. He seemed like some sort of actor in period clothes. Anyway yeah, I did have a couple of shots of wild turkey. But I'm ok. REALLY!"

Maddy smirked. "So, did you find out anything useful?"

Gary pulled the folded map out of his breast pocket and un-furled it, "Well Squeezle marked the location of the saloon and here's the Butterfly Lake Campground, so we're really close."

"Can you trust some Mountain Man with a name like Squeezle? I mean, who has a name like that?"

Gary in his alcohol influenced semi-stupor laughed. "Yeah, I know... But the bartender..."

Maddy interrupted, "Harry?"

"Yeah Harry, anyway he told me that Squeezle lives out there by Butterfly Lake, so I guess we can trust the guy... Besides, if you look on the map the only lakes close by are right there." And Gary pointed to the marks that Squeezle made on the map.

Then Gary perked up, "Where are the girls?"

Maddy looked up momentarily glancing across the street before pointing with her outstretched hand at the clothing shop, "Oh don't worry about them, they're in hog-heaven right now racking up some big bills on our credit cards. No worries."

Then she added, *"I'm getting hungry... maybe we ought to think about having some lunch somewhere?"*

Gary smiled, *"Yeah let's do that!"*

And they both stood up to cross the street to retrieve their daughters.

Lunch

Once they convinced the two girls to take a break with the promise of some decent lunch, the four of them walked down to the **Cast Iron Skillet** restaurant.

All the buildings on the main street were right out of some Old West Movie. The local city council members really spent quite a bit of time recreating what could have easily served as some Old West Movie Town.

As the four of them entered the restaurant a middle aged woman with a gingham apron approached them at the door.

She was using her apron to wipe her hands, as she smiled and said, *"Table for four?"*

Gary and Maddy both nodded and the waitress smiled before stepping over to the cash register to retrieve some menus.

Then she returned and said, *"That table by the window is open if you don't mind that damned dog staring at you through the window for a handout?"*

Gary frowned and said, "How 'bout that one?" pointing to an adjacent table.

Immediately the girls spoke right up, "Dad?" they said in unison as twins often do.

Gary smiled at the waitress, "OK. OK. That window table will be just fine."

The waitress smiled and walked over to pull the chairs out so the family could be seated. Then she said, "My names Gertie and if you have any questions just flag me down and I'll be right over."

And once the family was seated Gertie distributed the menus to each of them. Of course the two girls grabbed the seats that were closest to the window, so they could watch the dog outside.

Rach asked Gertie before she left, *"What's his name?"*

Gertie took a moment to respond, *"It's Sally... He's a She."*

After a moment staring out at Sally... Gertie chimed in, *"Her owner; Bert Parker, used to come in here every morning for breakfast, before he passed away... But Sally kept coming. Over the past few years, She's become a sort of institution around here so we don't chase here away. Usually the customers share their food with her, but if we notice that she's being ignored, we bring out something for her to eat, so she never goes hungry. OK. Take you time looking over the menu and I'll be back in a few minutes to take your orders, meanwhile... Can I get you folks some coffee?"*

Gary shook his head 'no' as Maddy asked, "You have any tea?"

Gertie answered, "I can bring you some hot water and a Lipton Tea bag if that's OK?"

Maddy smiled and answered, "That would be wonderful, thanks."

Then Gertie looked at the two girls, "You girls want something to drink?"

Melanie chimed in right away. "Can I get a small OJ?"

Gertie smiled and nodded. "And what about you young lady?"

Rachel spoke right up, "I'll have a coffee with cream and sugar."

Gary frowned, and when Maddy saw his response she added, "She's been drinking coffee for years honey."

Then she glanced at Gertie, There's a Starbucks® on every damned corner these days where we live. Kids. They grow up way too fast. Besides I'm betting you don't have a Starbucks® within a hundred miles of Dawson City?"

Gertie frowned and pointed with her outstretched hand, "There's one just down the street. My grandson drinks the stuff like water. You know we sell coffee for under a dollar with FREE refills, but the Starbucks® down the block charge a fortune for that stuff! Mostly it's the younger crowd that frequents the place. I mean, it's still just coffee, right?"

She paused and then added... "OK. I'll be right back with your beverages." And she walked away.

Gary spoke up, "The people here are real characters. Everyone is very nice. I wonder what it's like living in a town like this? Kind of like living in the Old West"

Maddy rubbed her face with her hand, "OK. OK. Wild Bill. Don't be getting any ideas, alright?"

Mel added, "Yeah dad. I don't think our family is capable of living way up here in no man's land. It's a nice place to visit but..."

Gary spoke right up, "Well, you haven't seen Butterfly Lake yet. Perhaps you'll like that?"

Rach chimed in, *"Not enough to move here."*

Everyone laughed.

The Lake

After their meal and after the girls were convinced that Sally was well fed a big syrup drenched buttermilk waffle and a strip of bacon, the family waited out front while Gary retrieved their vehicle, and soon they were on their way to the lake.

Gary guessed that the drive out to Butterfly Lake was no more than six or seven miles. But it wasn't too long before they crested a small hill and then the main lake came into view.

It was gorgeous to be sure. The actual site was actually made up of several smaller lakes that all seemed to be tied into the main body of water known as Butterfly Lake.

The smaller lakes did not show up on Gary's map but he was not deterred and he was glad that his family had finally arrived at their destination safely.

They passed through a very nice gateway that was right out of a storybook, and then within a mile or so they came to a small gas station, and a food store and next to it was a sign that read 'Bait Shop'.

Gary trying to get a laugh said, "*Oh look girls, your favorite thing... a Bait Shop!*" The twins frowned.

He drove up to the main building and found an elongated parking spot, and the family exited the vehicle.

Maddy immediately commented as she took in a big breath of mountain air, "*My God. That smells delightful!*"

He surmised that those elongated parking spaces were setup for small tour buses. However, the only vehicle parked there was an oversized van with the name **Butterfly Lake Resort** plastered on both sides.

Gary volunteered, "*Your mother and me will get us registered, but please don't wander off until we can all get the 'lay of the land', alright?*"

The twins answered in unison, "*Yes. Dad.*"

Gary and Maddy entered the main building and managed to locate the registration desk. No one was present so they rang the small bell on the desk.

Within a few minutes a geeky middle aged man came out from a back room with a white napkin in his hand, he began to wipe his mouth before speaking. "*Hi folks. Can I help you?*"

"Hello young man. I'm Gary Richards and this is my wife Madaline. Hopefully you have us on your books for a two week stay?"...Gary announced.

The man shoved the napkin in his back pocket and started to thumb through the registration book, "Richards you say?"

Gary smiled, "Yes. Gary and Madaline Richards."

"Oh yes. Here we go. Gary and Madaline Richards plus two youngsters?"...The desk clerk announced.

"Yes. That would be our twin girls." ...Gary confirmed.

The man asked, "If you wouldn't mind, can I see the credit card that you'll be using? I just need to verify the payment option."

"Oh yeah, sure." and Gary fished out his credit card and handed it to the man. The desk clerk verified that it was the same card number that he had on file, and he handed it back. Then he gathered all the rest of Gary and Maddy's pertinent information and within a few minutes, they were registered.

"Because you made reservations early on, I have you in a very nice campsite down by the main lake."

He smirked and held up his index finger to pass along some information that he surmised The Richard's might be interested in. "We had a large group of unusual characters roll in a couple of days ago, but I put them in a campsite far enough away because they seem to be a little rowdy."

"Gee, I hope that they aren't gonna be troublemakers." ... Gary asked.

"Naw. I don't think so. We get all kinds coming up here. We've had them all at one time or another. Even had some bikers show up one time. But usually they're all fairly well behaved. Sometimes they can be a bit noisy, but we've never had any real trouble out here." ...The desk clerk related.

Maddy asked, "But this place is safe, right?"

"Oh yeah. We're only a few miles from Dawson Creek, and the Sheriff and even his staff all come out here to fish. And when they do show up, they park their patrol cars right out front." And he pointed through the front window. "That's usually all that people need to see in order to be on their best behavior."

Then he retrieved a homemade map of the overall campground. "OK. You're here, and I've got you in a lakeside spot, here. It's easy to spot. You'll have no trouble finding it. I didn't see any requests for electrical power, but because of that other group... I'm putting you in a powered campsite at no extra charge."

Gary smiled, "I'm sorry but I didn't catch your name?"

"Oh I'm sorry. My name's Clem, and it's me and my wife Betty who run things out here. I also manage the Bait Shop which is open around 10 AM until 3 PM daily. I'm usually there unless someone is trying to register."

Clem smiled, "Oh. There's a laundromat onsite, but there's no one in there when it's operational. Everything is run on quarters, so if you need some change you'll have to come back to the registration desk and I'll make sure that you have some quarters, in case you need to do any laundry?"

There was a pause, then Clem said, "Well, I hope that you'll enjoy your stay. You could not have picked a better time of year for a visit."

"Oh. I don't know if you folks watch that Gold Rush TV series, but the producers always stay with us and sometimes even a cast member or two will camp with us." ...Clem explained.

Gary smiled, "My daughters are huge fans... and my girls did make all the arrangements to come all the way up here to Alaska to take that tour."

"Well. That's serendipitous because the tour bus leaves from our parking lot, out front." ...and he pointed out the front window. "So your in luck. You won't have far to go."

Gary and Maddy smiled, then Gary added, "Well. My wife and me aren't booked for that. Just my daughters."

Clem added, "Oh. That's a shame. It's really quite a tour. I think you and your wife might have liked it."

He paused, before adding, "OK. I think you're all set. And if there's anything that you need just come back to the office, or... the Bait Shop... I wear a lot of different hats around here and I might be over there... just grab me if you need some more help or you have questions?"

Then he added, "I'll have my grandson Gene walk you over to the campsite. He'll show you how to access the electrical service. And if you're gonna try your luck fishing... I can sell you a daily or weekly license. Obviously we also have a variety of bait for sale too. This time of year the Bass are biting like crazy, so you might like to try your luck? If you didn't pack some fishing poles, we have some that we can rent you. Just ask?" Gary and Maddy nodded, then Maddy thanked him for his help.

Getting Settled In

Gary and Maddy seemed to be pleased that the two girls seemed to be embracing the camping experience, at least that was how things appeared.

Surprisingly, the girls were still sitting in the car when Gary and Maddy left the main office. They were shocked that they didn't have to run around looking for them.

Once the task of unpacking was underway, the two girls started to become less interested, and they wandered off by exploring the beauty of the main lake.

As they were moving towards the water, Maddy yelled out, "Be careful down there girls, it a long walk back to Dawson City if we need to find a doctor."

Of course neither girl acknowledged what their mother had said.

Maddy just stood there watching her daughters as they moved down the embankment where they stepped out on one of several forty foot long floating docks that were placed up and down the shoreline.

The docks were spaced accordingly at every other campsite, and parked alongside many of them were various sized fishing skiffs adjacent to many of the campsites.

The brochure specifically mentioned that 'speed boats' were not allowed on Butterfly Lake. Canoes and Small Fishing Boats were the only floating devices allowed on the lake. And... the outboard motors that were connected to some of the smaller (less powerful) boats were small electric versions.

Obviously Water Skiing or any other Speed Boat activity was **NOT** allowed.

There were signs posted strategically both on the floating docks as well as a few posted on some select trees scattered around the campsites that outlined the rules and regulations of the resort.

As Rachel and her sister made their way out to the end of the floating dock adjacent to their campsite... they commented between themselves. Rachel said, "It is beautiful isn't it?"

Her sister replied, "Yeah. And that air. You smell that?"

"Smell what?" ...Rachel asked her sister.

Her sister just smiled, *"It's clean air for a change, and it smells great"*

That's when a voice came from behind them, *"What smells great?"*

Scorpio had joined the two girls on the floating dock. She approached so quietly that the two girls who were caught up in the moment didn't even realize that she had approached them.

Scorpio was wearing a halter top and some cutoff denim shorts. She was barefooted. Her body was well exposed which showed off the fact that her arms and legs were covered with tattoos.

The girls were startled.

"Oh I'm so sorry if I startled you girls. My apologies." …**Scorpio** volunteered.

Rachel grabbed her chest, *"No problem. We didn't hear you approaching that's all. I'm Rachel and this is my sister Melanie. Were the Richards! We just arrived today with our parents. We drove all the way up here to Alaska from California. In the United States?"*

Melanie sarcastically interrupted her sister's story, *"If we drove all the way up here to Alaska, she already knows that we came from somewhere in the United States."*

Scorpio smiled at this sibling revelry. *"That's OK. I figured that out. Me and my friends are from the 'States' as well."*

Rachel asked, *"What's your name?"*

*"They call me **Scorpio**. It's a nickname that seemed to have stuck, so that's what everyone calls me."* …**Scorpio** explained.

Mel inquired, *"Have you been here long?"*

"My associates and me arrived by motor home about a week ago." ...**Scorpio** explained.

Mel asked, *"I guess you're a fisher-person, huh?"*

"Heaven's no. My friends and me are up here in Alaska on business. However, two of the guys in my group did 'rent a boat' and they did go out one day to try their luck, but no... I personally have no interest in fishing." ..She explained.

Rach asked, *"Did they catch anything?"*

Scorpio answered enthusiastically, *"Actually yes, they did... and Clem's grandson Gene actually cooked a nice dinner for us on the campfire. I assume that you met Gene and his grandpa Clem?"*

Mel answered, *"Not yet."*

Rach was curious so she asked, *"Man, you must have a fortune invested in your tattoos? Their pretty."*

Scorpio frowned as she tried to give the two girls a decent answer, *"Yeah well. I was young and stupid when I got them. When you grow up you learn not to do dumb things. My advice to you girls, 'don't get tattoos'. They end up marking you for life."*

There was a pregnant pause in the conversation, and then **Scorpio** broke the silence, *"Well, it was nice meeting you girls, I need to be getting back. Be careful out here by the water's edge, it's over twenty feet deep out here at the end of the pier. Do you both swim?"*

Mel answered, *"Yeah we can swim."*

"OK, then. Take care." ...**Scorpio** responded as she made her way back towards the shoreline.

Once she was out of range Mel chimed in, *"Man. What a weirdo?"*

"Just because she has a few tattoos?" Rach asked.

"Come on. 'a few tattoos?' Except for her face and hands she's covered with them! She belongs in a side-show." ...Mel commented.

Rach laughed, "Despite the Tatts she seems nice enough?"

Mel could only shake her head at her sisters opinion. To her **Scorpio** was still a weirdo.

Setting Up the Campsite

Gary and Maddy were almost done unpacking everything from the car and trailer, and when Maddy saw the girls strolling back into camp, she was not too pleased. *"We could have used some help here. Where have you two girls been?"*

Rach spoke up, *"We were down by the lake just checking things out."*

Mel chimed in, *"Some woman came over and she was covered in tattoos. Needless to say, she was kind of interesting. She seemed 'out-of-place' way up here in no man's land."*

"Yeah. She kind of reminded me of someone who should be in a rock-&-roll band. I found her kind of interesting." ...Rach speculated.

"Hummmm?" ... Mel added.

After Dinner Conversations

Each campsite had a small cement sink that was plumbed with water... Ice Cold Water to be sure, but still useful enough that the twins were able to do the dishes without too much difficulty. It was located right next to an outdoor grill.

Mel inquired, *"I hope to God that we aren't expected to bath in that freezing water?"*

Maddy after overhearing her daughter complain retrieved the brochure and she began to read out loud, *"It says here that behind the laundry there's a separate Men's and a Woman's shower with hot water. It says that there's soap and shampoo provided, but if we don't have towels that we can pick up what we need at the front desk. It also asks us NOT to do any dishes in the shower."*

"What about a toilet?" ...Rach asked.

"Oh ah, this little map shows several restrooms that are situated every so often throughout the campground. And it says here that there's hot water in each of those. But they still ask that we don't wash dishes (or clothes) in there. It does say that we can clean fish in the cement sinks in each campsite, but they ask that we bury the fish scraps in the woods or burn that stuff in the campfire."

Gary chimed in, *"Did we pack a small shovel?"*

The two girls answered simultaneously, *"Yes dad!"*

First Night at Butterfly Lake

With no television... and as soon as dinner was concluded, and once the fireplace wood was all burnt up... the four of them crawled into two adjoining small tents.

Gary had forgotten to purchase a few bundles of firewood from Clem (and Clem forgot to ask). Except for the pre-stacked firewood that came packaged with the campsite his family was limited to the one campfire that first night, before having to go to bed.

He decided that the next day he'd have to buy a few bundles of firewood so he could keep the family happy.

He was worried that he was gonna have to be creative so his two girls didn't lose interest in camping altogether.

But once everyone was cozy in their goose down sleeping bags, it wasn't too long before everyone was sleeping like 'babes in the woods'.

As the girls were about to drift off, Rach asked Mel. *"By the way... Did you see any Butterflies?"* Before realizing that her sister was already asleep.

Buying a few Essentials

Gary was up rather early and mentioned to Maddy that he was headed over to the main office to see Clem about purchasing some bundles of Firewood.

He slipped on his clothes and made his way over to the main building.

No one was at the main desk, so he politely (and quietly) rang the bell.

By the second ring Clem finally emerged from the back room.

It was clear that he hadn't been up too long himself. He commented, *"You're an early riser I see? No matter, some of the fishermen are up at the crack of dawn. I guess it's time for me to get my butt in gear. How can I help you Mr. Richards?"*

"Good morning Clem, Yesterday I failed to buy some firewood, so when that initial campfire died down last night, we all just went to bed." ...Gary explained.

"Oh eh, sorry about that... I should have asked about that. My mistake. How many bundles would you like?"...Clem asked.

"Well, my kids would be upset if we can't keep a fire going until at least 8 or 9 pm?"... Gary explained.

Then he added. *"Just getting my girls to agree to come all the way up here to Alaska was like pulling teeth, so I need to placate them at every opportunity so they don't rebel. Kids. What us parents won't do huh?"*

Clem laughed at Gary's attempt to be funny. Then he said, "Well, it's easy to burn though 2 or 3 bundles a night, but as long as you're gonna be here for several days, may I suggest that Gene bring over a couple of wheelbarrows full of logs that should keep you going all week. We offer a discounted rate when you buy firewood that way, so you'll save some money instead of having to buy firewood by the bundle."

"Yeah, yeah... that seems like a better idea. That way I can help keep the peace." ...Gary suggested.

"Wonderful. I'll just add it to the credit card that we have on file."...Clem explained.

"*Great*" ..Gary agreed.

"*By the way, my two girls signed up for that Gold Mining Tour, and if I understood you correctly those tours start right out front in the parking lot? correct?*" ... Gary inquired.

Clem Smiled, "*Correcto Mundo! The tour bus comes by every Tuesday and Thursday. They meet with our guests right out front in the parking lot. Let me check to see which day that they have your daughters scheduled for?*"

Clem walked over to a scheduling book and looked up the Richards. "*It looks like you're scheduled for this coming Thursday, assuming that the weather is favorable. It's about an hour's drive out to the mining site, and then the tour takes a couple of hours, which includes a nice lunch that is furnished.*"

Gary turned to look out the window at the main parking lot... "*You said that they meet right out there in the parking lot?*"

"*Yep. You're gonna have to tell your girls that they need to be ready to go by 9 am on Thursday. The driver usually hangs out until ten or so, but they won't wait for too much longer, so the girls need to be ready-to-go... as close to 9 am as possible, just in case?*"...Clem explained.

Gary smiled, before asking, "*When does everything conclude?*"

"*Well. It's usually an all day trip that usually returns around four pm. Between now and Thursday, I hope to see you and your girls out on the lake to do a little Bass Fishing.*"... Clem suggested.

Gary turned to leave the office but before leaving he commented to Clem, "Yeah, getting my two girls into a fishing boat ain't gonna happen unless Pigs learn how to Fly. But my wife and I might want to take you up on that!"

Clem laughed. *"Your girls might surprise you?"*

Gary added, *"Not too likely."*

Both men laughed.

Boredom

By Wednesday Gary and Maddy had settled in to a life of relaxation, both of them were happy enough just lounging around the campsite.

But by that same time their two twin girls were out of their minds with boredom. Both girls had already hiked all the way around the big lake on Tuesday, which took them several hours.

By Wednesday Mel & Rach spent most of the day on the floating dock drinking sodas, visiting with Clem's grandson Gene, or swimming in the lake.

They seemed to be experiencing some difficulty keeping themselves occupied.

That same day Maddy and Gary actually purchase a couple of fishing licenses, and rented one of the small dinghy's from Clem at the Bait Shop with a small electric motor, and a couple of oars in case that electric motor gave up the ghost? The boat also came with two very adequate life jackets.

Another attraction was the well groomed trail that ran all the way around the lake.

Thankfully that trail was well used, and well within sight of the water, so getting lost was NOT too likely as long as guests stayed on the established trail.

Either hikers continued all the way around the lake, or... they gave up and backtracked on the trail until they found themselves back at the main parking lot which most guests ended up doing.

Only the youngest campers usually made it all the way 'round the lake.

Very few individuals made it all the way 'round the lake if they were not seasoned hikers. It was the teenagers who were full of, *'piss an vinegar'* that usually completed that task.

Most of the older folks gave up and found their way back to the trail head.

The countryside was still on the wild side. And if one ventured too far from the main trail into the dense woods there was no telling what you might encounter.

The area was rich with wildlife. Moose, Deer, Elk, and even Black Bears and Mountain Lions were abundant once you foolheartedly stepped too far into the dense brush and surrounding forest. That's when you could be taking your life in your own hands if you decided to wander off too far.

The Bait Shop rented Air-Horns which were highly recommended for hikers who wanted to venture around the lake. Those were recommended as a way to scare off any errant animals which were known to find their way to Butterfly Lake.

Every few years, a youngster lost his or her way and had to be rescued by local park rangers. Those Air-Horns were instrumental in helping to locate lost hikers.

In nearly a hundred years Butterfly Lake only lost one experienced hiker. Two youngsters who did not heed the waning signs that appeared on select trees every 100 feet or so, had to be rescued in the 1950's.

But since that time Butterfly Lake had a steller record and except for that one hiker, no one else ever went missing for more than a day or so.

If you could read English it was clear that a potential hike all the way around Butterfly Lake (which was estimated to be close to eight miles) could turn out poorly if you didn't heed the warning signs which preached to everyone... *"stay on the trail"*.

Also, carrying an Air-Horn with you was a great deterrent for animals that you might run into. And if you did experience some medical issue... The Air-Horn was a great way to get some much needed help.

Everyone who purchased an Air-Horn from the Bait Shop was diligently schooled how to use it, and each person was told that they could get 75% off their rental fee if the safety tape was still attached to the trigger and they returned it to the bait shop. Just blowing it off to hear how loud it was, was strongly discouraged. And, If you returned it with the original tape seal on the trigger guard, Clem & his wife Betty would issue a refund.

The Butterfly Lake brochure encourage everyone who was thinking about making the hike all the way around the lake to purchase an Air Horn as a preventative safety device.

Mel and Rach followed suit and at the encouragement of their folks, they purchased one for their hike. Of course they tossed it into one of their backpacks and quickly forgot that they even had it.

Thankfully with the exception of a few deer, some eagles, and some beaver their hike was uneventful.

When the girls gathered around the campfire that night they were both animated as they recounted their experience to their parents, who listened with great interest.

Gary asked his girls if they saw any butterflies, but neither had any response and a moment later the question passed as if he had never even asked.

He had started to wonder himself why the lake was called that... if there were no butterflies in that part of Alaska?

Entertainment Night

Wednesday was 'entertainment night' and when there were enough campsites rented out, Clem and Betty eiher hired a local band to perform on the little stage that was already setup near the parking lot, or they showed an old classic movie after dark with **FREE** buttered popcorn and complimentary sodas.

Sometimes they brought in a naturalist who spoke about the local area and related some pertinent history related to the Yukon Gold Rush, or Dawson City.

The little open air theatre was setup nicely with a bunch of fairly comfortable benches cut from fallen trees.

This is also where they held music shows too. Gary and Maddy thought how charming everything was. Of course their girls tried to remain aloof. Nothing about Butterfly Lake was going to impress them enough to leave it's mark. They would see to that!

When the family arrived this particular Wednesday evening around 7:30 PM they spotted **Scorpio** and her motely crew of misfits. Even the girls (let alone their folks) thought **Scorpio** and her friends seemed a little bit 'out of place'. They didn't seem like people who were interested in camping.

In any event, a local Rock-A-Billy Band by the name of the 'Overtime Boys' provided the music on Wednesday.

There was a small 20 x 20 foot dance floor between the stage and where the bench style seats began, and a few folks made good use of that during the music portion of the show.

By 9 PM everything concluded and attendees began to make their way back to their respective campsite's.

During the show **Scorpio** did wander over to meet the girls parents to say hello. But she cut her visit short and had very little to say before rejoining her friends.

Gary did comment that he thought that she and her buddies seemed out-of-place, and Maddy seemed to agree. But **Scorpio's** visit was so brief that no one referred to her again.

Maddy 's only comment was that she thought that she was a very unusual woman with all those tattoos and spikey hair. She referred to her as an enigma.

Soon the family was calling it a night, as they made their way back to their campsite.

Besides, tomorrow was the big day for the Gold Rush Tour, and The Girls were committed to be in the parking lot by 9 AM to get on the tour bus.

Continental Breakfast

Clem and Betty had setup several tables and chairs next to the parking place where the tour bus would be located.

They furnished a nice Continental Breakfast that included coffee, hot chocolate, donuts, and pastries from a local bakery in Dawson City. The Gold Rush Tour Company routinely paid for these embellishments.

Will Furlough the bus driver addressed the small audience at 9:40 am. *"Hello everyone. My name's Will Furlough and I'll be your bus driver today. We'll be departing around 10 am. Now here's a few things that are important to pass along."*

"Yes, we do have a small restroom <u>on the vehicle</u>, that's B. U. T., and <u>not</u> B U T T ". (**Everyone laughed**)

"And although you're welcome to use it, we hope that you will try to make at least one more pit stop <u>here</u> while you still have a chance."

He paused as this news sunk in to the heads of the guests before continuing.

"The trip out to the actual claim where *Gold Rush* is filmed is about an hour's drive. About every five miles the tour company has set up 'port-a-potties' along the roadway and we encourage you *'get my attention if you need to use the restroom.* If you get my attention and use one of these port-a-poddies, then I don't have to clean the restroom on the van later, and I can get back home an hour or so, earlier." (**Everyone Chuckles**)

"If you can last until we arrive at the mining camp they do have a very nice restroom onsite with flushable toilets. And please excuse me for mixing talk about restrooms with talk about lunch."
(**Everyone Laughs**)

"The tour company has made arrangements to provide a wonderful BBQ Brisket lunch with Garlic Bread and a baked potato for everyone before we begin to make our way back to Butterfly Lake. Well. At least **I think the lunch is wonderful!** (**Everyone Laughs**)

"Usually we end up making a number of pit stops on the way home depending on how spicy the BBQ Sause is?" (**Everyone Laughs**)

"So, please don't eat too much as the ride home can be little rough! And the less you eat, the bigger my tips." (**Everyone Laughs**)

He takes a look around at all the guests.

"Also. If you see some wildlife, I will stop the van... but please don't ask to get out of the vehicle. Just get my attention and I will pause the van so everyone can take a picture or two out the window. Remember the animals that you see are WILD. Yes, they can be the cutest things that you're probably ever gonna see... but they're WILD ANIMALS, so as cute as they seem... they're dangerous animals and we don't want you to end up in the BBQ SAUCE like the last group of tourists!" (**Everyone Laughs**).

"If you decide to ignore my advice, I can assure you that it's <u>a long walk</u> back to Butterfly Lake, and there's no hitchhiking allowed in Alaska! Up here we only have the BEAR necessities." (**Everyone Laughs**)

"OK everyone... Let's get this show on the road?"

Will stands by the steps and greets each guest with a smile and a handshake as each tourist gets onto the bus. The guests line up and soon each of them is seated in the van. That's when Will climbs aboard and positions himself in the driver's seat. He straps on a microphone that is position so that he doesn't have to hold it (as he drives).

"Testing, testing... 1-2-3-4, testing. Can everyone hear me?" ... Will asks.

Then he rotates so that he's facing the guests... "OK. So... this mother skunk is out foraging in the woods with her to skunk sons. One is named 'IN' and the other is named "OUT". (**Everyone Laughs**)

"Anyway, at the end of the day while the mother skunk is fixin' dinner, she discovers that her son 'OUT' is the only one that comes home. Becoming worried, she asks her son 'OUT" if he can go back into the woods to retrieve his brother 'IN'. About an hour passes, and finally she notices that 'OUT' has returned with his missing brother. The mom is amazed and asks her son how he found his brother, and 'OUT' takes a big breath and then says... with confidence... 'IN STINKED!" (**Everyone groans, before laughing**)

Will joins the group in laughter. "OK folks that's about as good as the jokes are going to get, so try to enjoy them." (**Everyone Laughs**). Then he adds, "There are seat belts on every seat, and you'll be happy to have them on when we hit some of Alaska's famous pot holes. Remember this is the only road in and out of the mining camp, so it can be a little bit bumpy."

Soon everyone is strapped in and Will starts up the van and within minutes they're off on their tour.

It isn't too long before Mel leans over and asks her sister... *"Seems kind of weird seeing that* **Scorpio** *woman and her friends on this tour, don'tcha think?"*

Rach glances back to where the motley crew has taken up residency near the back of the van. *"Hummmm? Maybe their fans of the Gold Rush Show?"*

"Hummmm. I don't know Rach they don't look like people who would watch a show on TV like Gold Rush?" ... She volunteered.

"Hey look, isn't that a Bald Eagle?" just then Will slows down before adding his commentary, "Off to your left is one of Alaska's State Chickens, eh... Eagles... sorry!" (**Everyone Laughs**)

About twenty minutes into the excursion Will points out the first set of two 'Port-A-Poddies' situated on a pull out alongside the one lane dirt road. He starts to slow down, before asking, "Anyone need to stop? It's another five miles to the next oasis."

He doesn't get any takers, so he adds... "OK put a cork in it until we get to the next rest area." (**Everyone Laughs**)

He pauses for a moment and then Will begins to tell another joke, "So this cop is sitting on the side of the road when a speeding pickup truck passes him at a rather fast pace. When the guy is finally pulled over, the cop makes his way up to the driver's window. As he does he notices that there are a bunch of Penguins in the bed of the guys truck."

"After discussing the guy's speed and coming to an agreement that he should 'take it easy'... The cop asks... 'Oh, and one more thing, what's the story with all the Penguins? "

The driver smiles and explains that they 're his friends and that they're *just out for a 'ride and some fresh air'.*

The cop says, "Well, you ought to take those animals to the zoo."

"The next day the cop spots the same speeding truck and when he catches up with the guy, he gives him a second warning about his speed. Then as he makes his way back to his patrol car. That's when he notices that each Penguin has a pair of sunglasses on."

"So, he returns to the driver's window to speak with the driver one more time... Yesterday I thought that I told you to bring all those Penguins to the zoo?"

"The driver seemed surprised and he immediate answers", *"I DID!"*

Then the cop asked, "So, what's with the sunglasses?"

"The driver explains, *"Well officer. Today we're going to the beach!"* (**Everyone Laughs**)

Will takes a quick break 'telling jokes' and announces, *"We're just about twenty minutes away folks, so hang onto your britches."* (**A few guests chuckle**)

It isn't too long before they *crest* a final hill and down below they get their first glimpse of the mining camp in all its glory through the front windshield of the van.

Suddenly **PINK** stands up and makes his way to the front of the van, where he pulls out his pistol and points it at Will, telling him, *"Pull Over."*

Obviously Will is shocked, but he does what he's told.

As the van roils to a stop, **PINK** motions with his pistol, *"Your phone?"* and he curls the fingers of his left hand indicating that Will should comply.

Will tries to stall, and he smiles sarcastically at **PINK** , *"You must realize that there's no phone service out here right?"*

PINK speaks with a commanding voice. *"Look we know that you have a Satellite Phone dipshit, so give it up or there will be consequences."*

71

Will tries [a second time] to answer, but before he can get the first word out, **PINK** shoots him in the leg.

Everyone on the bus is shocked at the loud pistol report. Will let's out a grown as he grabs his right leg.

PINK unhooks Will's seat belt and drags him out of the way and he drops to the floor in pain. Then **PINK** slides into the driver's seat to take over.

A rather large guy sitting near the back of the van begins to stand up, but **Scorpio** taps him on the back of the head with her pistol, telling him, *"Sit your fat ass down motherfucker."*

Black stands up and walks towards the front of the van to address the guests.

"OK everyone, Listen up. If you cooperate no one else will get hurt."

A guest in his fifties who happens to be sitting in the first row on the right side of the van, next to his wife... Suddenly seems to tighten up and he attempts to stand up, saying, *"You bastard!"*

Immediately **Black** shoots the ceiling of the van, and that guy immediately falls back into his seat in shock. Then **Black** looks at the vigilante and says, *"Now don't make me kill you pops! Cause I will."*

The guy's wife grabs him by the shoulder to console him. To make sure that he doesn't do something stupid and die a hero. *"Harold please, don't do anything stupid?"*

Black continues, *"OK. If everyone behaves, no one else will get hurt."* Then he motions towards **Fool** who comes to the front of the van and he steps down into the wheel well holding his weapon for all to see.

Black continues, "Everyone just sit tight. We're not here to harm you folks, we didn't come here to rob you. We're after some bigger fish."

Pink puts a finger up to his lips to indicate that **Black** is giving away too much information."

Black smiles at him and nods. Then **Black** asks the guests, to help drag Will towards the back of the van to an empty seat located to the rear of the van.

Scorpio makes her way towards the front of the van past Will to join her friend **Fool**, making sure that every guest see's that she is well armed.

Rach leans over and whispers in Mel's ear, *"Can you believe this? I knew that there was something weird about that* **Scorpio** *woman."* Mel can only shake her head in disbelief.

As the van creeps into the mining camp on the main road, some guy appears in the middle of the road, waving at the van, he's all smiles.

Scorpio who was watching out front as **Pink** navigated the van into the main parking area. Asks, *"Who the fuck is that guy?"*

All the way from the back of the van Will volunteers an explanation. *"That's Steve Williams, he's one of the producers of the show. He meets us out here for every tour."*

As the van slowly creeps into the main parking area, Steve is all smiles, as he walks over to the van... and once he reaches the doorway **Pink** opens the door and Steve steps in squeezing past **Scorpio** and **Black**.

Both had the good sense to keep their weapons hidden from view. **Scorpio** drapes a light duty windbreaker over her UZI as she deposits her Glock® in her belt behind her back.

Steve is so enthusiastic that he doesn't even notice that Will is not behind the steering wheel as he climbs aboard.

Black pulls out his pistol and shoves it against the temple of Steve's head. *"Welcome aboard my friend. So glad that you could join us."*

Steve is shocked and asks, *"Where's Will?"*

"Back here Steve!" ...Will yells.

Steve hears him and turns, and **Scorpio** pushes him down the isle towards some empty seats in the back where Will has been deposited.

She takes a seat across the aisle from the two men keeping her UZI trained on both of them.

Steve asks, *"You alright Will?"*

"I got shot, so no... goddammit, I'm not alright, OK? Those assholes shot me. Thank God the bullet didn't hit any bone." ...Will explained.

Steve immediately stood up and said... *"There's a first aid kit under the dash can someone get it back here so I can address this guy's wound?"*

Will gave him a concerned look. And Steve immediately announced. *"Don't worry I was a Medic in Nam... Piece of cake. It's literally just a flesh wound."*

"You sure about this?" ... Will asked.

"Yeah, yeah, I'll have you good-to-go in no time once we get the blood flow to stop." And Steve looks over towards **Scorpio**, *"If that is permissible?"*

Scorpio nods but doesn't say a word. As Steve gors to work on Will's injury.

Finding the Gold

Once the van is maneuvered to its normal parking spot, everyone is herded off the bus into an area with at least a half dozen park style benches. This is where the lunches are normally served.

Several cooks and servers are working the tables, and despite everyone's shock and awe, a wonderful lunch of Beef Brisket, French fries, and Green Beans is served to the entire group.

Pink, **Black**, **Fool** and **Scorpio** make their sinister presence known. **Scorpio** drags Steve Williams off the van and out into the open under gun point, *"Where's the safe located?"*

Steve reluctantly points towards the *'clean up shack'* before adding, *"But Chris or Parker aren't here and they're the only people who know the combination."*

"Don't worry your pretty little head about that... **Fool** *can crack the combination in no time. That damned safe is just a flimsy consumer model, it ain't gonna keep us from getting inside."* ...**Scorpio** explains.

Rach and Mel have taken up seats at one of the picnic tables across from the man that seemed to be interested in taking control much earlier on the van.

Rach opens her backpack and at the same time that she taps the man's hand to get his attention.

He looks over and seems a bit bewildered, and then she slides the Air-Horn from her backpack slides it over to this man. He looks around suspiciously before pulling the Air-Horn into his lap covertly. He looks down to see what she had given to him, and gets a proper grip on it, while he tears off the safety tape from the trigger.

The man fumble a moment too long and Fool smells a rat, so he walks over, *"What the hell are you fumbling with asshole? STAND UP!"*

As the man stands he feigns a foot injury as he carefully attempts to stands up erect next to the bench. As he does, he acts like he's having trouble complying and he reaches down to rub his leg.

Fool asks, *"What the fuck is wrong with you asshole? I said stand up!"*

The man answers, *"I'm sorry. I was injured in Viet Nam and sometimes my right leg doesn't seem to work properly."*

Fool makes the mistake of reaching over to help him stand up, and like a bullet the man brings the Air-Horn directly up to Fool's ear and he depresses the button.

A sudden blast of noise enters **Fool's** ear and **Fool** immediately drops his weapon, grabbing his head with both hands... yelling in pain, *"Ahhhh,!"*

Immediately the man picks up **Fool's** Glock and he shoots him several times dropping him where he stood.

Then he immediately shoots at **Black** who catches two bullets before dropping to the ground. **Black** is injured but not deceased and he returns fire, killing the Good Samaritan.

As **Black** lays there in agony, **Scorpio** walks over and finishes **Black** off. Pink rushes over and asks Scorpio, "What the fuck?"

She points her Uzi at **Pink** and says, *"You want to drag his ass home after this? Besides... it just means that there's more gold for the two of us."*

Pink takes everything in, and after some thought he nods then he turns to face the tourists as he raised his weapon in a threatening manner. *"Keep your seats motherfuckers! We don't want to kill anymore of you hero's then we have to. Behave yourselves and you'll live to be able to tell your grandkids what happened here today!"*

Steve Williams after witnessing the bloodshed is visibly shaken. **Scorpio** walks over and she grabs him by the knap of his neck and she throws him towards **Pink**, *"Take him to the safe?"*

Pink, & Steve Williams with **Scorpio** in tow as she scans the seated tourists with her weapon.

She walks backwards behind **Pink** and Steve, towards a small building where the cleanup usually happens, and where the safe is located.

She moves the barrel of the Uzi back and forth as she points the menacing weapon towards the seated crowd.

Then she announces to the tourists. *"Now we don't need any more hero's. Just sit there and behave yourselves and enjoy your lunch. If you try anything stupid, that Steve guy... inside, is history! You all know what we're capable of, so behave!"*

Some of the more terrified tourists begin to nibble at their lunch. But no one is really hungry anymore.

Inside the cleanup shack **Pink** smiles as he gets a load of the safe that contains several seasons of gold recovery. He looks at Steve, and tells him, "Take a seat and behave, if he wants to see another day?"

Steve sits down across the room from **Pink**. He has no desire to try to do anything but comply.

Pink laughs as he sizes up the safe. He asks Steve, *"A gun safe? That's the best you could do to safeguard millions of dollars' worth of gold? You do know that these gun safes were just designed to keep normal people honest, right?"*

Steve was amazed when Pink brought out a stethoscope and began to fiddle with the combination lock.

Within no more than 10 or 12 minutes... he cracked the combination and pulled the heavy door to the safe open. He yelled loud enough so that Scorpio who was still sitting outside on a bench (watching over the group of tourists) could hear him. *"OK. It's open!"*

Scorpio stood up and opened the door a crack so she would be able to communicate with **Pink** while she still kept her Uzi trained on the group out front. *"Is the gold in there?"*

Pink was staring at several stainless steel thermos style bottles along with a 5 gallon plastic bucket with no lid. That bucket was almost filled to the brim with gold.

He lifted one of the smaller bottles and noticed right away that it was extremely heavy.

He unscrewed the cap and spilled out a palm sized sample of gold granules' that fell into his palm. **Pink** smiled before looking towards the open door where **Scorpio** was still standing. *"OK. It's here just like **Architect** said."*

Immediately **Scorpio** pulled out a satellite phone from her vest and she called **Architect.** He answered immediately and *asked... "Report?"*

"Success. Come and get us the hell outta here! ...She almost demanded.

Architect immediately said, *"Fifteen minutes, tops!"*

About seven minutes later the sound of the chopper could be heard approaching as it made its way towards the mining operation.

Once the chopper was on the ground **Architect** addressed the crowd as he picked out several of the largest men at gun point (including Steve) who were tasked to transfer all the gold from the safe into the chopper.

Within 10 minutes the safe had been emptied.

They figured that they had close to six million in Gold at today's prices. **Pink, Scorpio**, and **Architect** climbed aboard the chopper and soon they were putting on one of several headsets as **Architect** maneuvered the chopper in the air making a clean escape from the crime scene.

Architect noticed right away that **Black** and **Fool** were not present. He asked, *"What about **Black** and **Fool**?*

Scorpio answered, *"They didn't make it."*

"Did you happen to retrieve their weapons?' ... **Architect** asked.

Scorpio shook her head, 'no'.

Then **Pink** chimed in, *"They fucked up!"*

Within ten minutes **Architect** swooped down close to the surface of an Alaskan Lake, and he looked at the remaining two crooks and said, *"Everything goes. Weapons, Clothing, Everything... get rid of it! There's a duffle bag back there with a set of fresh clothes for the two of you. Put your old clothing inside, and there's a 10 lb. bar bell back there, put it into that duffle bag and throw everything overboard."*

"But not the gold right? ...**Pink** asked.

Scorpio gave him a surprised look, *"Are you that fucking stupid? Of course not the Gold."*

He just smiled at her, knowing full well that he was just fucking with her.

Scorpio shook her head, *"Fuck you, you prick."*

He laughed.

At the Airport

As the chopper approach the airstrip the three crooks could see a small private jet waiting on the tarmac.

Nearby was a huge black limousine.

As **Architect** sat the helicopter down two Saudi men got out of the limo and they leaned on the side holding onto their headdresses as the helicopter's rotor finally came to a stop.

The men from Arabia were joined by three others from the waiting jet, and soon all of the gold was transferred over to the plane.

As **Architect**, **Pink** and **Scorpio** moved towards the limo which was supposed to be their ride out of the area, one of the two men from the limo pulled out a pistol and began shooting at the three.

Thankfully **Architect** had a pistol, and he shot both of them immediately, then he began shooting at the jet that was beginning to roll down the runway.

"Are you fucking kidding me? Those bastards are ripping us off!" ...Scorpio yelled.

Pink ran over to the guy who was shooting at them, and he retrieved his handgun to join **Architect** in lobbing some lead at the retreating jet. Of course the handgun fire was inconsequential, and the jet took off.

The three of them just stood there... shocked at what just happened.

Pink spoke up first. "I hate those fucking rag heads."

Architect shook his head in disbelief. **Then Pink asked**. "I thought you said that those assholes could be trusted?"

Architect said, "All is not lost. Let me contact the main people who helped set this heist up. I need to find out why this happened?"

Then he asked **Scorpio** and **Pink** to help him put the two dead bodies in the trunk of the limo. Once inside they left the airport and that's when **Architect** tried calling his Arabian contacts.

"Hakeem what the fuck my man? Your guys tried to kill us." ... **Architect** asked. "A coup, are you fucking with me?"

"No what remains of my team is in the limo, and two of your people are in the trunk. No. Their dead." ... **Architect** revealed.

"OK. OK. So now what? Yes, your jet is on the way, with the gold. So where does that leave us?"

Obviously the guy at the other end of the telephone call is attempting to explain things.

Architect interrupts... "No that's unacceptable! 60% is not going to work for us! You initially offered 85% of current prices. I lost two good people on this heist... Yeah, yeah, OK. You lost two people as well, but those guys were part of some coup, so we did you a big favor by icing them. It's a case of tit-for-tat. No I already said that 60% is not doable. He covered the receiver with his hand and pulled the limo over to the side of the road where he turned to address **Pink** and **Scorpio**.

"They want to offer us 75% of current value.

Scorpio said, "Tell them we'll accept 80%."

"We'll accept 80%, and no more fucking monkey business... I trusted you guys and I expect you to live up to your word."

There was a long pause as the guy on the other end began to respond.

"OK. OK. But don't fuck with us! OK. Then we have an agreement? OK, yeah I think we're good. But don't fuck with us." ... **Architect** replied.

He addressed Pink and Scorpio, "OK. I think everything will turn out alright."

Scorpio spoke right up. *"I hope so, because those tourists were snapping pictures of us on their iPhones left and right. Were gonna be on tonight's 6 o'clock news. If we don't get that money, and find a safe haven, we're fucked."*

Architect spoke up. "Well the first thing that you two need to do is get the hell out of the country. I can help you accomplish that."

*"I'm not leaving without my fair share, and I think **Pink** and me should each get what you promised to **Black** and **Fool**. All this fucking bullshit has to be worth that - at the very least."* ...**Scorpio** emphasized.

Yeah I have no problem giving you both the extra shares. No problem." .. **Architect** explained.

"OK. As long as those assholes pay up?" ...**Pink** suggested.

"After 911, the Saudi's can't afford any more bad publicity. So, I think we're good." ... **Architect** speculated.

"How much do you think we'll both earn?" ...**Pink** asked.

"Somewhere around two million to each of you once the Saudi's payout the promised percentage." ... **Architect** speculated.

Scorpio started to reveal some unnecessary information regarding her locaion. "Well, I'm headed to South America. I ought to be able to live like a queen on that kind of money."

Pink spoke right up, *"Well I ain't about to tell you two where I'm going, but it ain't South America, that's for sure."*

Architect shook his head, *"Look I don't care where you go, in fact I don't want to know. This job is my last heist. We've all come away with a fortune that should last us a lifetime, as long as we keep our mouths shut, and behave."*

Pink nodded in agreement, and **Architect** smiled and added, *"We did really good. You can be sure of that. This heist will go down as one of the biggest that ever happened."*

Finally, the Cops Arrive

It seemed like hours before the authorities finally arrived, it was way after dark. The local authorities setup additional outdoor lighting, as EMTs took Will away for medical treatment, and the local coroner took away the dead.

> It was rumored that Parker Schnabel was flying in to access the situation, but he wasn't expected to be there anytime soon as he was filming another series, "**Parker's Trail**" elsewhere. Fortunately for Parker, he had insurance to cover his losses.

Thank God the lives lost consisted of two of two of the perpetrators, and one exceptional fellow who tried to be a good Samaritan.

> It was estimated that the thieves got away with almost nine million in gold.

Oh, and... Unfortunately Will (the tour bus driver) who suffered that leg injury after being shot early on stopped driving for the tour company.

Mel and Rach were glad to see their parents who drove out to the site to pick the girls up.

Clem and Beatty; who were following the story on the local news, indicated to Gary and his family that they were certainly under no obligation to stay at their campsite any longer than they wanted to, and they volunteered to give the family a full refund.

Gary refused saying that it was no fault of Beatty or Clem. He appreciated the kind gesture, but he wanted no part of any refund. However, the family did pack up the next day and decided to head home early.

At the robbery site, Maddy was crying her eyes out and Gary held back his tears of relief when he saw the two girls again and was reassured that they were both unharmed.

As Gary and Maddy approached the girls came running.

"My God girls, I am so, so, glad that you're both OK." ...Maddy announced as she hugged her daughters.

Mel began to cry when she saw her parents arrived and she wouldn't let go of her mother. Rach seemed a bit stoic.

Both girls knew that this was something that they would NEVER forget for the rest of their lives. It was certainly a 'life changing' experience.

Mel looked over towards her father, before announcing, *"We should have gone to Yosemite."*

Gary smiled and said... *"Maybe next year."*

Mel smiled and added, *"But NO CAMPING!"*

The family laughed.

Reliving the Details

Under the circumstances Gary and Maddy (and the two girls) were allowed to vacate the campground early by Clem and Beatty.

Everyone (by that time) had been appraised of what went on that day at the mining site as it was plastered all over the local news.

Will recovered and gave up his position with the tour company. In fact mining tours were cancelled altogether after that... indefinitely.

Rach seemed to be the more effected of the two girls. The murders really stuck in her mind, and Gary wondered if she would ever recover from that experience. She never spoke about it again.

The authorities track the culprits

It took almost two years for the authorities to track down **Pink**. He had setup shop in a mountain enclave near Alberta Canada, when they finally caught up with him.

He was living large on the nearly two million that was deposited by the Saudi's into a special offshore bank account.

He did not go down without a fight and the Alberta Police killed him in his luxury home. He had applied for a Canadian driver's license and it was from that photo that witnesses who were at the mining camp identified him.

Scorpio lasted a little longer in Bolivia where she had setup shop. Her squeaky white Anglo appearance eventually called way too much attention to her, but it was her lavish spending habits that really called attention to her. She had visited a local tattoo artist and he was soaking her 'big time' for a bunch of new tattoos that he was commissioned to create for her.

Architect who managed to take almost four million from the heist, although finally identified... had managed to disappear forever.

The authorities never had a single lead that amounted to anything substantial. He remains a fugitive to this day.

The heist went down as the largest haul in history.

Peter Schmitt's name (yes, he was finally identified as the mastermind of this heist) his name was became synonymous with the name of another crook - **D.B. Cooper** as a couple of crooks that actually got away it.

A s the years moved forward Mel finally attended college and turned out to be a rather normal woman.

Rach on the other hand became quite withdrawn and never left home. She became a recluse, and somewhat unsocial. Almost ten years to the day, she took her own life.

Gary and Maddy were extremely broken hearted and blamed the perpetrators of the heist for ruining their daughter's life.

Gary eventually retired from the law firm and him and Maddy never spoke about what happened to Rach again. Chico e3ventuslly died of old age, and they picked up a second Golden Retriever from the pound, which they named **Chico2**.

Eventually they started calling her "Two".

Mel eventually met a nice fellow and after two years of marriage... she made her folks grandparents with a cute little fellow that they named Will after that brave tour bus driver.

She and her husband eventually moved to a small town in. Oregon... *"Bandon by the Sea"*

Consuelo remained with the family until her husband Hugo passed away from complications from his diabetes.

Eventually Consuelo passed away and by that time Gary and Maddy decided to move into a much more manageable home in Norther California near Shasta Lake. The location allowed them to make weekend trips to see their daughter's family.

Sometimes Gary and Maddy would just sit quietly on their front porch sharing some homemade lemonade.

They must have had the heist on their minds but it was something that they never spoke about.

THE END

ABOUT THE AUTHOR...

Denny has been a creative author for decades. As of 2024 he's amassed an impressive collection of approximately 80+ short-stories and books that are published by **Amazon.com** and **Audible.com** in the following genres. Your invited to visit his website to review his work at: **dennymagic1.com**.

...Kelly Singleton – Publicist

Brass Belle Literary Publishing. - New York, New York

- **Lifestyle**
- **Westerns'**
- **Children's**
- **Love Stories'**
- **Supernatural**
- **Crime Dramas'**
- **Science Fiction**
- **Historical Fiction**
- **Woman's Stories'**
- **Period Adventures'**
- **Controversial Expose's**
- **Mystery & Supernatural**

Made in the USA
Middletown, DE
26 January 2025